S0-BUB-095

6 7 8 06 05 04

Produced by Mega-Books of New York, Inc.
Design and Art Direction by Michaelis/Carpelis Design Assoc.

Cover illustration: Don Morrison

SUPER STAR

by Judy Katschke

interior illustrations by
Marcy Ramsey

STECK-VAUGHN
C O M P A N Y

CHAPTER ONE

It was a typical evening on Planet DomE in the 25th century. Comets streaked across a red-violet sky. Steam spouted from craters. The temperature was a comfortable 459°. And fifteen-year-old twins LisandrA and NinandrA had to answer to their mother.

"No, Mom," LisandrA sighed. "NinandrA and I don't have dates tonight."

"It's just that the guys in school are either grunts or geeks, Mom," NinandrA insisted.

"I don't want to hear anymore," their mother groaned. "I'm going to my Mars-Jong game."

"Have fun, Mom!" the twins said together.

Their mother paused at the front door. "Surely there's one boy on this planet who meets your high standards!"

"There is, Mom!" NinandrA called out as their mother left the living chamber. "Except he's not on this planet!"

LisandrA gave her twin a quick shove. "Crater mouth!" she hissed.

"Okay, okay!" NinandrA sighed.

LisandrA walked over to a silver cabinet, and pressed a red button. The cabinet doors swung open. Inside was something more precious than gold: the family hologrameter!

The entertainment device created three-dimensional pictures, or holograms, right in the twins' own living chamber. The hologrameter even allowed them to watch holograms of movies from Planet Earth. LisandrA began to program the voice-activated hologrameter. "The planet we want is

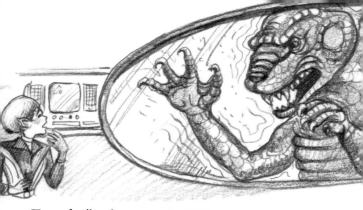

Earth." she said. "The category is Movies. The year is 1958."

"Here!" cried NinandrA. "Let me enter the code word!" She grabbed the hologrameter. "The code word is lizard!"

"No!" screamed LisandrA.

It was too late. They heard a loud roar. The twins ran to the window of their dwelling ship. Outside, the giant lizard, Radzilla, was thundering over towards them.

LisandrA groaned at her sister. "The code word isn't lizard! It's gecko, like his name! Johnny Gecko!"

"But a gecko is a lizard, isn't it?" asked NinandrA. "Sort of?"

"Give me that!" said LisandrA. She erased Radzilla just as he was about to put his giant claws into their window. She quickly entered the word gecko.

A shimmering ball of light appeared. Suddenly, there stood Johnny Gecko. His black hair was gleaming.

"Hiii, Johnny!" called the twins. They knew this wasn't the real Johnny and that he couldn't hear them, but they didn't care.

They sat back and watched the three-dimensional scene from Johnny's famous movie, *Love Me Something Awful*. Wearing the tight gecko-skinned pants he was famous for, Johnny sang and swiveled.

"Gorgeous!" moaned LisandrA.

"Drop-dead gorgeous!" sighed NinandrA.

"Why couldn't all the guys on Planet DomE be like Johnny Gecko?" sighed LisandrA.

CHAPTER TWO

The next day the twins entered the busy Sustenance Hall at school. They slumped down at a table and took out their lunch: purple plasma in pitas. Their conversation was interrupted by a loud laugh.

The twins looked up to see RobertO, the school's one hunk. He was sitting at a nearby table surrounded by girls. At the end of his table was AndrO. AndrO had a major crush on LisandrA. The feeling was not mutual.

"Look what he's doing to AndrO." NinandrA whispered to her sister.

RobertO was tossing donuts onto AndrO's antenna while the girls sitting

around the table chanted the count.

"Three! Four! Five!"

LisandrA and NinandrA watched as AndrO sat motionless under a cloud of powdered sugar.

"Why doesn't he do anything?" NinandrA asked LisandrA.

"Because he's too embarrassed to get angry," LisandrA said. NinandrA nodded. It was a well-known fact among Planet DomErs that their anger created powerful increases in strength.

Just as RobertO was about to toss another donut, LisandrA leaped from her chair.

"This is sick!" she said. LisandrA was filled with the the extraordinary power of an angry DomEr. She marched over to RobertO. With a slight tap on his shoulder she sent him reeling back in his chair.

"Hey!" cried RobertO. "What's your problem?"

"Right now it's you!" shouted LisandrA. She motioned for NinandrA to join her as she stormed out of the Sustenance Hall.

"You were great!" laughed NinandrA as the twins strutted down the hall.

"Yeah, you were incredible!" The twins turned to see AndrO, following behind them.

Underneath the powdered sugar on

his face was a sugary look of love. LisandrA reached out and yanked a donut off his antenna.

"I just hate to see good donuts go to waste," LisandrA shrugged.

As the twins continued to walk down the hall, AndrO called out, "Hold on! Wait! Don't go!"

"Why not?" asked NinandrA as she and her sister turned around.

"Because there's a secret I want to share with both of you," AndrO answered.

"Spare us," LisandrA sneered.

"No!" cried AndrO. "My secret is something amazing! Something astounding! Let me show you!"

The twins stared at each other and shrugged. They followed AndrO to an empty classroom.

"Okay. Astound and amaze us," said LisandrA.

"It's in my backpack!" AndrO said excitedly.

The twins watched as AndrO pulled out a square metal box. It had knobs and switches on its front and sides. On the top was a blinking red light.

"What is it?" asked NinandrA.

"It's a birthday present from my Aunt," smiled AndrO. "Meet the Super Duper!"

"The Super Duper?" asked LisandrA. "What does it do?"

"It duplicates just about anything in the universe!" said AndrO proudly. "Here. Allow me to demonstrate!"

AndrO reached over and pulled NinandrA's meteor-rock ring from her finger. He then placed it on a desk.

"I just point the Super Duper at the ring," AndrO explained, "then I turn the dial and flick this switch!"

LisandrA and NinandrA watched in

15

awe. The ring was bathed in a brilliant light. When the light faded, two rings stood in the place of one!

"Wow!" the twins exclaimed.

AndrO gave the rings to the twins. "See? Now you both have one!"

"How does it work?" asked NinandrA.

"I'm not totally sure. It might have something to do with the separation of molecules . . ."

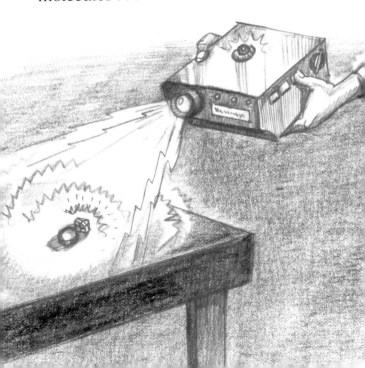

AndrO's speculation was interrupted by the buzz of a large fly. LisandrA grabbed the Super Duper.

"My turn!" She aimed the box at the buzzing fly.

"Don't!" cried AndrO. "Please don't!"

Without even looking, LisandrA spun the dial and flicked a couple of switches. The brilliant light appeared again, this time over the insect. Suddenly the room was filled with a whirring swarm of flies.

"Whoops!" laughed NinandrA.

"Oh great!" moaned LisandrA, swatting the flies with her hands.

LisandrA grabbed the donuts and tossed them out of the window, one by one.

"Maybe they'll go after the donuts!" she cried. "Fetch!"

"What we really need is something to go after them," said NinandrA.

"Like what?" asked LisandrA.

"I don't know! Maybe we should dupe

a fly-eating lizard!" NinandrA suggested over the buzzing. "Or a gecko!"

LisandrA turned to stare at her twin. "What a brilliant idea!" she gasped.

"She grabbed NinandrA's hand and pulled her out the door. LisandrA gave her twin a sly smile. "I know just the gecko we're going to dupe! Earth, 1958, here we come!"

CHAPTER THREE

"I don't know, LisandrA," said NinandrA. "I'm not sure this is such a good idea!"

"A Johnny Gecko for each one of us is not a good idea?" cried LisandrA. She carried the holgrameter over to the sofa where her twin was sitting.

"But how will we get to Earth in the year 1958?" asked NinandrA. "And how will we get our hands on a Super Duper?"

"You handle the time-travel arrangements," explained LisandrA. "I'll handle AndrO."

LisandrA flicked a switch on the holgrameter. "Now, if we're going to visit Earth in the 1950s, we'll have to do some research."

"Are you calling up the Earth History category?" asked NinandrA.

"No," answered LisandrA. "I'm calling up 1950s Television Shows!"

The twins sat back and waited for the holograEmeter to spring into action. Soon a smiling woman with a plate of cookies appeared in their living chamber.

"I know you two have a busy day in school," the woman said. "So I baked you your favorite Crispy Treats!"

"Cool!" cried NinandrA. She reached out for a cookie but her hand went right through the dish.

"She's a hologram. Remember?" sighed LisandrA.

"What's that thing she's wearing around her waist?" asked NinandrA.

Suddenly a clean-cut boy appeared next to the woman.

"Good afternoon, Mrs. Cheever," he

said. "My! That's a lovely apron you're wearing today!"

LisandrA gagged and zapped the two holograms out of their living chamber.

"What's next?" asked NinandrA.

"Oh, my gosh!!" screamed LisandrA. "Look! Help!"

They were face to face with a furry long-haired creature with four legs.

"What is it?" shrieked NinandrA. The sisters clutched each other in fear.

The creature was suddenly joined by

21

a tearful little blond boy.

"Oh, Sassie!" he cried, hugging the creature's neck. "I thought you were lost in the forest fire!"

"Are you sure you want to go to the 1950s?" whispered NinandrA.

"Yes!" snapped LisandrA. "We're going for Johnny, not Sassie!"

Two hours later NinandrA walked into a small office to take care of her share of the task.

"Welcome to Partners-in-Time!" smiled CarA, the time-travel agent. "What can I do for you?"

"My sister and I want to travel to Earth in the year 1958," said NinandrA.

"Earth? We have a special this week!" beamed CarA. "The Salem Witch Trials, 1692!"

NinandrA knew her Earth history. She imagined herself and LisandrA being dunked in a pond or tied to a stake.

"No, thanks," NinandrA shuddered.

"Next week there'll be a special on the

Jurassic Period!" added CarA.

NinandrA could practically feel the hot breath of a giant Earth dinosaur in her face. She shook her head politely.

"All right then," sighed CarA. "Fabulous Fifties it is."

NinandrA watched as the time-travel agent beamed two tickets through.

"Now," CarA continued. "Would you care to arrive in Los Angeles, New York, Dallas . . ."

"Pinkerton, Kentucky," NinandrA

said firmly. She looked serious.

CarA gawked. "What is there?"

"A good friend," NinandrA answered.

CarA sighed as she handed NinandrA the tickets. "Enjoy your trip!"

Meanwhile, LisandrA sat on a hill with AndrO.

"I'm so glad you agreed to watch the meteors crash with me, LisandrA," AndrO said.

"I just couldn't resist," LisandrA forced herself to say. She turned to look at AndrO's backpack resting nearby. By its bulk, LisandrA knew it held the Super Duper.

AndrO reached into his pocket and pulled out a small telescope.

"What is that thing?" asked LisandrA.

"It's a meteor tracking device," said AndrO. "Would you like to look through it?"

LisandrA hesitated. "No, thanks," she said. "I'd rather have my own."

"No problem," AndrO shrugged. "I'll

just dupe it for you."

LisandrA jumped up and grabbed the backpack. "I'll do it. It's time I learned how to work a Super Duper!"

AndrO wasn't paying much attention to his backpack. There was something much more important on his mind.

"LisandrA, about the Big Dipper Dance that's coming up," he stammered.

"Will you go with me?"

LisandrA rolled her eyes. "I knew that was coming," she thought to herself. Then she turned to AndrO and smiled.

"I'll think about it, okay?" LisandrA called over her shoulder as she ran off with the backpack.

"Hey! Where are you going with my Super Duper?" cried AndrO.

"Don't worry!" answered LisandrA. "You'll get it back!"

"Wait!" AndrO shouted. "You forgot the instructions!" He stared down at his hand. "And the meteor tracking device!"

CHAPTER FOUR

"Are you sure we'll look like 1950s Earthlings when we land?" LisandrA wanted to know as she and her twin boarded the time-travel ship.

"Relax!" said the steward. "As soon as you get to your destination, your domed heads will shrink and your ears will round out. You'll pass!"

"What about our antennas?" asked LisandrA.

"Earth is a lot cooler than Planet DomE so your antennas will shrink neatly into your heads!" the steward explained with a smile.

The twins gulped.

"Will our clothes be transformed,

too?" asked NinandrA.

"Of course!" the steward said. LisandrA and NinandrA carefully placed AndrO's backpack with the Super Duper under the seat. "Once on Earth, how do we get back to the ship?" LisandrA asked.

"You just click your heels and say, 'There's no place like DomE!'" the steward laughed. The twins looked at each other and rolled their eyes.

"Now, if you'll fasten your safety belts," the steward continued, "the captain will be ready for blastoff!"

The twins felt a strong vibration. As the ship traveled, a screen flashed the names of the planets it passed: Saturn! Jupiter! Mars! And finally, Earth!

"Next stop, Pinkerton!" called the steward cheerfully.

The twins stared at each other, then at the screen. It flashed: Pinkerton, Kentucky. 1958.

"Grab the Super Duper!" NinandrA

remembered just in time. The twins began to spin like cyclones. Suddenly they screeched to a halt.

"LisandrA!" cried NinandrA. Your ears are round, your head is small . . . and your antenna is gone!"

"You don't look so hot yourself!" cried LisandrA.

The twins were dressed in lavender poodle skirts, frilly blouses, and saddle shoes. The backpack with the Super Duper was now a Sassie lunch box.

"I hate lavender!!!" shouted LisandrA as they were sucked out of the ship.

The twins opened their eyes and the first thing they saw was a sign which read, Honeysuckle Street.

LisandrA reached for the lunch box.

"How do we know if we're in the right town?" asked NinandrA.

LisandrA pointed to a banner hanging across the street. "That's how!" *Pinkerton welcomes its own Johnny Gecko!* was printed on the banner.

The twins jumped up and down in excitement. NinandrA stopped to point at a round dome filled with smaller colorful domes.

"LisandrA!" she hissed. "Isn't that someone we know?"

They ran to the bubble gum machine and began shaking it. Pulling up the metal flap, they shouted into the opening. "Hello! Hello! Are you from DomE?"

The twins didn't see a woman with

flaming red hair come out of the neighboring beauty shop.

"Either it's the heat or your ponytails are too tight!" she said, wobbling on high heels. "You twins aren't from these parts, are you?"

"Um . . . no," said LisandrA.

"We came to see Johnny Gecko," smiled NinandrA.

"I knew it!" cried the woman. "You must be the girls from *Teen Scream* magazine!"

The twins shrugged and nodded.

"I thought the contest winners were meeting Johnny in New York City!" the woman said.

"Contest winners?" asked LisandrA.

The woman held out a hand with long orange fingernails. "I'm Ima Jean. Allow me to be your hostess in Pinkerton!"

"I'm LisandrA."

"I'm NinandrA."

"Lisa and Nina!" said Ima Jean. "Pleased to meet you!"

The twins shook Ima Jean's hand and followed her into the shop. LisandrA leaned toward NinandrA. "From now on we're Lisa and Nina, got it?" she whispered to her sister.

Ima Jean's Beauty Shop was decorated in shades of pink and baby blue. French poodle dogs with top hats sprinkled the wallpaper. Pinned onto the wall were cuttings from fashion magazines.

"I'd like you girls to meet my daughter, Florence," Ima Jean said. "But you can call her Flo!"

She lead the girls to a teenage girl sitting under a hairdryer. The girl's face was covered with a mint green mask and her hair was wrapped around pink plastic rollers. The twins wondered whether Flo was an alien, too.

"Flo, say hello to the winners of the *Teen Scream* contest!" smiled Ima Jean. "They're the lucky girls who get to interview Johnny Gecko tomorrow!"

Flo glared at the girls, then at her mother. "Shoot, Mama!" she snapped. "It should have been me! After all, I'm the Pinkerton Homecoming Queen."

Ima Jean turned up the heat on Flo's hairdryer, making her squirm.

"Hush up!" whispered Ima Jean. "I've decided to welcome those girls into our home for the next few days."

"Why?" cried Flo, sweating under the dryer's heat.

"Because this could be fine publicity for our beauty parlor, that's why!" hissed Ima Jean.

"Okay!" cried Flo, ducking out from under the dryer. Whipping off her plastic cape, she strolled over to the twins.

"Aren't you a little old to be carrying that, honey?" she asked Lisa sweetly.

"What?" asked Lisa.

"That!" snapped Flo. She nodded toward the floor. Next to Lisa's feet was the Sassie lunch box.

"No!" said Lisa coolly. "Nobody is too old for Sassie!"

"Yeah!" Nina agreed. "He's our hero!"

Flo laughed wickedly. "Boy! Wait until Johnny finds out he has to be interviewed by two space cadets!"

"Did she say 'space cadets?'" Lisa murmured to her sister.

"You don't suppose she knows?" whispered Nina, "do you?"

CHAPTER FIVE

That night in Flo's bedroom, the Homecoming Queen was showing off all her Johnny Gecko souvenirs to the alien twins.

"I don't suppose you girls own a Johnny Gecko princess phone?" Flo asked with a sneer.

"No," answered Nina. "We talk on a communicator which magnifies the image of the caller—"

Lisa gave her twin one of her usual quick shoves. "Nope. No princess phone," Lisa added.

The twins flipped through the pages of Flo's Johnny Gecko scrapbook. Flo had a great collection of pictures.

"Look!" said Flo. She pointed to the picture of a chubby woman handing Johnny a pie. "That's Johnny's mama, Ethel!"

"His mama!" sighed the twins.

The twins knew that nobody meant more to Johnny than his mother. She even played the role of his mother in the movie, *Mama*!

"One day I'm going to have my own

Johnny Gecko convertible!" said Flo.

"One day we're going to have our own Johnny Geckos!" Lisa mumbled.

The next day was the day all of Pinkerton had been waiting for: Johnny Gecko was to drive his salmon-colored convertible into Pinkerton Square!

That morning, Ima Jean had surprised the twins with complimentary makeovers at her beauty shop.

"Just tell everyone your hair was done at Ima Jean's!" she instructed them carefully.

While Ima Jean painted Flo's toenails, the twins sweated under the hairdryers.

"Lisa!" whispered Nina.

"What?" asked Lisa.

"Did your antenna pop up?"

Lisa stuck her hand under the hood and gasped.

"Oh, great!" Lisa whispered. "They were supposed to stay inside our heads!"

"The heat did it!" cried Nina.

"Shhhh!!" Lisa warned.

Just then the telephone rang and Ima Jean hurried to answer it.

"He's here??" she screamed into the phone. "Thanks, LaVelda!"

Ima Jean hung up the phone and turned around. "Girls! Johnny's convertible has been spotted just outside Pinkerton!"

"Mama, we've got to get to the square

now!" shrieked Flo. "I want to be right up front!"

Lisa and Nina stared at each other.

"We're not dry yet!" the twins cried out. They looked nervous.

Flo grabbed her mother's hand. "Who cares about them! Let's go!"

"Just slam the door on your way out!" Ima Jean called over her shoulder.

Ima Jean ran after her daughter. The twins ducked out from under the dryers and raced to the mirror.

"They can't know we're not Earthlings!" cried Nina. "What are we going to do?"

"I don't know!" shrugged Lisa in despair.

Over the mirror was a magazine photo of a woman. Her hair was piled high on top of her head. "BEE A HONEY WITH THE NEW BEEHIVE," read the words across the page.

Lisa handed her sister a comb. "Start teasing!"

Fifteen minutes later the twins were breaking through the crowd at Pinkerton Square. Johnny Gecko hadn't yet arrived.

"Let us through!" screamed Lisa. "We're the girls from *Teen Scream*!"

People turned to gawk at the twins' towering hairdos. They had never seen such high hair before!

A man fell to the ground laughing.

"Duck and cover!" he shouted. "Those girls have missiles on their heads!"

The twins approached the stage just as the Pinkerton High School Glee Club was finishing their rendition of "Blue Moon of Kentucky."

The chorus filed off the stage. The mayor of Pinkerton stepped up to the microphone.

"I understand we have some contest winners here today!" he smiled.

The twins jumped up onto the stage next to the mayor. He sputtered when he saw their towering hairdos.

Nina leaned toward the microphone. Her hair completely blocked the mayor from view. "Our hair was done at Ima Jean's!"

"No! No! That's a lie!" Ima Jean shouted from the crowd.

Ima Jean's voice was quickly drowned out by a nearby marching band.

"Yes, indeed folks!" stammered the mayor, stepping out from behind Nina's

hairdo. "I believe Johnny Gecko has come home!"

The people roared as the salmon-colored convertible made its way through the crowd.

"He's here!" Lisa screamed. "He's really here!"

"Oh my gosh!" cried Nina.

A hush fell over the crowd as the car pulled up to the stage. The car door opened. Out stepped Johnny Gecko.

CHAPTER SIX

The twins had to hold each other up as Johnny swaggered onto the stage.

"It's good to be home," Johnny purred into the microphone.

Every girl in the crowd screamed.

"Johnny," the mayor said. "Your neighbors of Pinkerton would like to present you with this!" He picked up a large stuffed lizard with jeweled eyes.

"Thank you kindly," mumbled Johnny, taking the stuffed animal.

The mayor wiped sweat from his bald head. "Johnny!" he called. "How about a song?"

The twins practically fell into a trance when Johnny stepped up onto the stage.

He picked up the microphone.

"Okay, that was the fun part," whispered Nina as Johnny adjusted the microphone. "Now, how do we get Johnny alone to dupe him?"

"Easy," Lisa smiled at her twin. "We'll tell Johnny we get to interview him for *Teen Scream*. Then we'll just let the

Super Duper do its stuff!"

The twins gave each other the DomE 'pinkies-up' sign. Johnny began to sing.

"It's got to be unlawful,
The way I love you something awful!"

At noontime, Lisa and Nina were nervously awaiting Johnny in the high school gym. It was Johnny's choice to

meet them there. He wanted to shoot some hoops during the interview.

"Where is he?" Nina whined.

"He'll be here," said Lisa, clutching the Sassie lunchbox.

"We do know how to work that thing, don't we?" asked Nina.

Lisa didn't answer.

"We do have instructions," Nina asked, raising her voice, "don't we?"

They heard a thumping sound coming from the hall. It was getting louder and louder.

"What's that?" whispered Nina.

"I don't know," said Lisa.

The door swung open and there stood Johnny Gecko. He was dribbling his very own gecko-skinned basketball.

"You've got the questions," he mumbled. "I've got the answers."

"Great!" Lisa laughed nervously. "And, boy, do we have a lot of questions!"

"Shoot," said Johnny, tossing the ball through a hoop.

Lisa nodded toward her sister to start the interview.

"Um . . . *Teen Scream* wants to know," Nina stammered, "why is salmon your favorite color?"

Johnny jumped around the basketball court as he mumbled an answer.

With shaking fingers, Lisa opened the Sassie lunchbox. She pulled out the Super Duper.

"What was it like working with your mama in *Mama*?" Nina asked with a shaky voice.

Lisa ducked under the bleachers. She carefully aimed the Super Duper at Johnny.

"Stand still!" Lisa whispered under her breath. Johnny was skipping around the court, dribbling the basketball.

"Do it already!" Nina hissed at her sister. "I'm running out of questions!"

Lisa held the Super Duper out in front of her and felt for the switch. She flicked it.

"Way to go!" cried Nina. "You did it!"

They watched Johnny transform into a large ball of glowing light.

When the light finally vanished, two Johnnys stood in the place of one!

"It worked!" screamed Lisa. "One for you and one for . . ."

Suddenly a third Johnny appeared.

Then a fourth and then a fifth!

"What's going on?" Nina gulped.

The twins watched in horror as ten Johnnys stood on the basketball court.

Nina grabbed her sister by her shoulders. "What was the Super Duper set for?"

Lisa checked the number setting.

"Remember the day we duped the fly?" Lisa asked slowly.

"Yeah?" asked Nina.

"Remember how many flies . . . "

Nina stared at her sister.

"Oh, no!" cried Nina. "You never reset the counter!"

Before Lisa could answer, more Johnnys filled the school gym. Fifty! Sixty! Seventy!

"What are we going to do with all these Johnnys?" cried Lisa.

Eighty! Ninety!

Soon one hundred Johnny Geckos stood staring at the twins.

"Um . . . hi," Lisa gulped.

The Johnnys turned on their heels and began swaggering out of the school gym.

"They're leaving!" screamed Nina. "What do we do?"

"Grab a Johnny and let's get out of here!" cried Lisa.

Slipping on the scuffed floor, the twins dashed out of the gym. They saw the Johnnys parading down the hall.

One Johnny stopped and turned around. He winked at the twins and blew a kiss before turning a corner.

"That's the Johnny I want!" Nina yelled to her sister.

"Let's get him!" cried Lisa.

They whizzed around the corner and saw a Johnny hunched over a water fountain.

"There he is!" whispered Lisa.

Nina emptied a wastepaper basket, snuck up behind Johnny, and brought the basket down over his head.

Johnny stumbled as the girls dragged him into a nearby classroom. They shoved Johnny into a chair and shut the door.

"Take that thing off!" Lisa ordered her sister. "He looks stupid!"

Nina carefully lifted the basket and screamed. Johnny had fangs!

"Oh my gosh!!" shrieked Nina. "It looks like the Johnny from *I Was a Teenage Bloodsucker.*"

The ghoulish teen idol snarled and lunged at Nina.

"Don't you touch my sister!" growled an angry Lisa. She marched over to

Johnny. With a DomE-strength tap on his shoulder she sent Johnny flying out of an open window.

The twins slammed the window shut. From there they could see the other Johnnys filing out of the schoolyard, into the streets of Pinkerton.

"That monster was not the same Johnny we saw in the hall!" Nina insisted. She looked confused.

"Maybe we didn't just dupe Johnny Gecko," Lisa shrugged.

"What are you talking about?" asked Nina.

"Maybe we duped Johnny's movie characters. You know, the different roles he played!"

"You think the Super Duper can do that?" asked Nina.

The twins checked to see if the coast was clear. Then they carefully slipped out of the school.

On their way down Honeysuckle Street, Lisa grabbed her sister's arm. She pointed inside a fancy restaurant. There was a Johnny dining with a shy-looking Pinkerton woman. He handed her a rose and kissed her hand.

"Johnny the Continental," sighed Lisa.

There were more Johnny spottings as the twins passed other restaurants.

They stopped in front of a pizza parlor. "It's Ima Jean!" shouted Lisa.

Ima Jean waved to the girls. The

twins watched as another Johnny placed a steaming pepperoni pizza in front of Flo's mother.

"That's the one from *Johnny the Singing Waiter*!" groaned Lisa.

Ima Jean pointed to Johnny and winked at the twins.

"If only she knew!" cried Nina.

The twins were interrupted by a loud roar. They turned to see a motorcycle rumbling down the street. The motorcycle was driven by a Johnny dressed in a black leather jacket.

"Well, what do you know!" groaned Lisa. "It's the Johnny from *Burning Rubber Rebel*!"

Lisa groaned even louder when she saw who was sitting behind the driver.

"Hey, you two!" shouted Flo. "May the best girl win . . . and I'd say she already has!"

"Okay," Nina said as the motorcycle roared off. "So far we duped an evil Johnny, a bunch of romantic Johnnys

and a rebel Johnny."

"Yeah, so?" asked Lisa.

"So, I hope we duped a good Johnny, too!" cried Nina.

They passed a senior citizen center. Through the window they could see a Johnny square dancing with a group of beaming silver-haired ladies.

"Don't worry!" said Lisa wearily. "There's a Johnny Gecko for everyone!"

CHAPTER SEVEN

"Take the aliens over to the jail!" snapped the police sergeant. *"Question them and get some answers!"*

Lisa and Nina were watching *Earth Under Seige*. They had ducked into the Pinkerton Palace movie theatre to hide from their awful mistake.

"Do you think they'll do that to us?" whispered Nina.

"What?" asked Lisa. She was still clutching the Sassie lunchbox.

"When they find out we're aliens," said Nina, "do you think they'll drag us to jail and . . . "

Suddenly they heard a scream. The lights went up.

"Children! Children!" Ima Jean was running down the aisle with her purse swinging around her elbow. "Run to your mamas! Johnny Gecko is a bloodsucking vampire!!"

The children in the audience screamed. They leaped from their seats and ran from the movie theatre.

Lisa and Nina stared at each other.

The vampire Johnny must have gotten to Ima Jean!

"Did he bite you?" Lisa asked, running up to Ima Jean.

Ima Jean shook her head. "Thank my lucky stars we were in a pizza parlor!"

She reached into her purse and pulled out a shaker can of powdered garlic. "I warded him off with this! Vampires hate garlic!"

Ima Jean began sprinkling the movie theatre seats.

"Let's get out of here," mumbled Lisa.

The twins bolted out of the theatre. They had to adjust their eyes to the powerful sunlight.

The first thing they saw was a crowd of people surrounding a man with grey hair. The name Jack was sewn on his workshirt.

"I don't care if he's a movie star!" shouted Jack. "That Gecko boy just robbed my cash register and he's going to pay!"

A senior citizen spoke up to Jack. "Don't you dare talk about Johnny that way!" she hollered. "He's a lovely boy!"

The twins inched their way past the arguing crowd.

"Norma Sue used to be my girl!" snarled a teenage boy. "Until Gecko got to her!"

A little girl was sitting behind a crate selling "I Kissed Johnny" buttons. About two dozen women were lined up to buy them.

"Those Johnnys didn't waste any time!" Lisa said to her sister.

"Listen!" said Nina.

A loud roar filled the air. All of a sudden, a dozen motorcycles made their way down the street. Each one of them was driven by a Johnny Gecko.

"There's more than one of 'em!" whistled Jack.

"My stars!" gasped a woman with a baby carriage.

They watched the motorcycles zoom

over the hill and disappear.

"Oh, it's that silly television show, '*Nosy Camera!*'" the senior woman laughed nervously. "Come on you all! Smile!"

A man dressed in a white lab coat broke his way through the crowd. "It's the result of atomic experiments, that's what it is!"

"Whatever it is, it isn't natural!" shouted Jack. "I say we destroy all those Johnnys!"

The twins looked at each other and bolted from the crowd.

"If they destroy all the Johnnys," Nina panted as she ran, "they'll destroy the real Johnny, too!"

"If only there was a way we could de-dupe them!" cried Lisa. "We've got to contact AndrO!"

They ran around the corner and slammed into another person. They smiled to see that it wasn't an Earthling. It looked like a fellow alien!

The creature looked up from the ground. It had a large, bubbly blue head and a single eye on its forehead. Its hands were long and web-like.

"You're an alien?" Lisa smiled.

"Only on Saturdays!" The creature

reached up and pulled off his head. Under the rubbery mask he was indeed just another teenage Earthling.

The boy handed them a sheet of paper. "Take one!"

The paper read, "Is there life on other planets? Find out at the Pinkerton Planetarium."

"Next year, I'm flipping burgers!" the boy vowed as he pulled the alien head back on.

The twins waited until he was gone.

"What do you think?" asked Nina.

"I think this place might be the closest thing to home!" said Lisa.

Moments later the twins were inside the Pinkerton Planetarium. Seated in the Galaxy Auditorium, they stared straight up at a star show twinkling on the domed ceiling.

"The universe," came the voice of a breathy announcer. "Our gateway to the future!"

"My neck is killing me!" moaned Lisa.

The auditorium was empty except for the twins and a snoring man. The rest of the town was too busy tending to the Johnny problem.

A six-foot projector rotated in the middle of the auditorium. It pointed to different stars and planets on the ceiling.

"I think I see Planet DomE!" cried Nina, pointing up at the ceiling.

"Don't get excited," said Lisa. "It's just a movie."

"Is it?" asked Nina.

Making sure the man was asleep, Nina crawled into the projector pit.

"What are you doing?" asked Lisa. She grasped the lunchbox and followed her sister.

"Help me aim this thing at DomE!" said Nina, grabbing the projector.

"I'm not strong enough!" wailed Lisa.

"Then get mad about something!" Nina suggested.

All Lisa had to do was think of Flo on that motorcycle with Johnny. Lisa gripped the projector and thrust it in the direction of DomE. The planet came into view.

"Now, let's activate our antennas and concentrate on AndrO," said Nina.

The twins shut their eyes. Their antennas buzzed loudly, causing the sleeping man to stir.

Suddenly, in the middle of DomE a

blurry image appeared. It was AndrO!

"Hello?" he called.

"AndrO!" yelled Lisa. "It's LisandrA and NinandrA. We're calling from Planet Earth!"

"Earth?" cried AndrO from the ceiling.

"We need to know if the Super Duper can reverse a dupe!" said Lisa.

"You bet!" smiled AndrO. "How do you think I got rid of all those flies?"

Lisa and Nina gave each other a hug.

"Could you tell us, please?" Lisa begged.

"Sure," AndrO shrugged. "Now, listen carefully. There's a yellow light on the right side. Next to the light is a knob. Twist the knob until the red arrow points to zero. Then aim and fire!"

The twins studied the Super Duper.

"That's all?" cried Lisa.

"Well not quite!" AndrO smiled. "There's just one more thing you have to do, LisandrA."

"What?" asked Lisa.

"Tell me you'll go to the Big Dipper Dance with me!" AndrO said shyly.

Lisa spoke from the corner of her mouth. "I'm still thinking about it."

AndrO's image began to fade away. "Okay! But don't forget to return my Super Duper!"

Lisa rolled her eyes.

"We still have to figure out how to round up all those Johnnys!" Nina sighed when AndrO was gone.

The twins noticed that the snoring man was now wide awake. He was on his knees, peeking out from behind a seat.

"Can you get Superman on that thing?" he called out.

CHAPTER EIGHT

It had grown dark by the time the twins reached Ima Jean's house.

Ima Jean was sitting on the sofa with a box of tissues on her lap. She was watching the *Bill Donovan Show* on a flickering black and white television set.

"Five women engaged to Johnny Gecko?" Bill faced the camera with an exaggerated shrug. "He's out of this world!"

"They're everywhere!" sobbed Ima Jean. "Everywhere!"

Lisa and Nina tiptoed upstairs. They opened the door to Flo's bedroom. There was Flo, lying on her bed, dressed in a black leather jacket. She was

painting her nails a fire-engine red.

"A hundred Johnny Geckos!" she laughed. "And I'm ready for all of them!"

The twins were not in the mood to listen to Flo. They slumped down on the floor and grabbed the Johnny Gecko scrapbook. They looked worried.

Nina opened the book. The first page held the picture of Johnny's mother, Ethel. Lisa looked over her shoulder.

"Nobody means more to Johnny than his mama!" Lisa said out loud.

Then Lisa jumped up and faced Flo. "Where did you see the movie, *Mama*?" she asked the girl.

At the Pinkerton Drive-In," said Flo, "Why do you want to know?"

Lisa didn't answer. She grabbed the Sassie lunchbox and Nina's hand.

"They just have a silly movie," Flo sniffed as the twins ran from her room. "But I have the real thing!"

***

The Pinkerton Drive-In wasn't hard to find. Its large, white screen was visible from every point in town.

"I don't see anyone around," said Nina. She checked in all directions.

"Everyone's out Johnny hunting!" Lisa replied.

"It looks like that includes the drive-in's projectionist!" Nina said as she opened the door to the hut marked "Projection Booth."

Inside the hut was a machine with two metal arms. Behind it were shelves filled with flat, round cans.

The twins smiled when they found a special shelf of Johnny Gecko movies.

"*Johnny Goes to Rome, Beach Towel Johnny, Not Enough Girls,* and *Mama!*" Lisa grabbed the last can off the shelf.

"Now what do we do?" asked Nina opening the can.

"We take the reel of film and feed it through the projector over there!" smiled Lisa.

Nina was impressed. "How do you know all this?" she asked her sister.

"I saw *Johnny Goes to Hollywood!*" Lisa grinned.

In no time the black and white film was rolling. Through a small window the twins could see the movie flickering on the huge screen.

"Now we go outside," Lisa said, picking up the Sassie lunchbox, "and wait for Johnny."

The twins sat huddled near the movie screen. The parking lot, usually filled with cars, was empty.

Lisa nudged her sister. "Hey, this is my favorite part!"

It was the scene in the movie where Mama is crying for Johnny to come home from the Civil War.

"Mama needs you, son!" sobbed Mama. "I can't go on without you!"

Nina took out a handkerchief and blew her nose. "Poor Mama!"

"Ever since you've been gone," cried

Mama. "The days are slower than molasses in January!"

"She's such a good actress!" cried Lisa. Tears ran down her cheeks.

Suddenly they heard the faint sound of male voices.

"Mama?"

"Is that you, Mama?"

The twins turned to see a parade of Johnnys coming out from between the trees. They were walking through the parking lot.

"I'm sorry I gave away your puppy, son!" Mama wailed from the huge screen.

"That's alright, Mama!" blubbered several Johnnys. "That's all right for you!"

As the drama grew heavier, the number of Johnnys grew larger.

Soon the twins were looking out over a sea of sobbing Johnny Geckos.

"Come back to me, son!" bawled Mama. The Johnnys fell to their knees.

Lisa opened the Sassie lunchbox and pulled out the Super Duper.

"Do it!" sobbed Nina.

"Okay!" sobbed Lisa.

Lisa followed AndrO's instructions. Then she turned on the Super Duper on the Johnnys and flicked the switch.

The twins covered their eyes from the blinding light. When the light finally faded, they peeked out from between their fingers.

"Look!" cried Lisa.

In the parking lot was a single Johnny Gecko.

"I'm home, Mama," he said to his movie screen mother. "I'm home!"

The twins looked at each other and smiled in relief.

"Home sounds good to me!" sighed Lisa. Nina nodded her head.

"There they are!" shouted a man. "Those are the girls who contacted Outer Space!"

The twins looked to see the man from

the Planetarium. He was followed by Jack and a gang of teenage boys.

"Come on, boys!" called Jack. We're hunting aliens, now!"

The men jumped over Johnny and charged toward Lisa and Nina.

"What will we do?" screamed Nina.

"I don't know!" cried Lisa. "What did the time-travel steward tell us to do?"

"Something about clicking our heels!" said Nina. The twins frantically banged their feet together. Nothing happened.

"We have to say something, too!" remembered Lisa. "Something like, 'There's no place like Rome!' Or was it Nome? Or . . . "

"DomE!" shouted Nina. "There's no place like DomE!"

Just as the men reached the movie screen, the twins began whizzing around. As they whirled, they felt themselves being sucked up.

"Whoaaaaa!!" they screamed.

The men looked up with gaping

mouths as the twins shot up into the night sky.

"Well, ain't they the possums that gumshoed the polecats!" whistled Jack.

The twins opened their eyes and smiled. It felt good to be LisandrA and NinandrA again. It felt even better to be in the time-travel ship going back to Planet DomE!

"How was your trip?" the steward asked the twins.

"I'll stick to the Twenty-fifth Century," said LisandrA.

"And Planet DomE!" laughed NinandrA.

Their domed heads and pointy ears had returned. The Super Duper was back in AndrO's backpack.

"I hope AndrO isn't planning on taking this to the dance," said LisandrA.

"You're going with him?" asked NinandrA.

"Sure," Lisandra said with a shrug. "After one hundred Johnny Geckos, one ordinary guy on Planet DomE is starting to look awfully good!"

The steward wheeled a cart of lunch trays in front of the twins. "Like I said, there's no place like DomE!" he said. "Now, will you be having the chicken or the purple plasma?"